This Book Is Dedicated To Everyone With A Dream!

Once upon a time, in the snowy mountains of Frostasia, lived a little penguin named Flipper...

Flipper was no ordinary penguin!
This wasn't going to stop him,
Nothing would hold him back!

Flipper grabbed his coat, packed his lunch
and was ready to go.

He waved goodbye to his penguin pals and waddled on his way...

He was going to do it!
He was going to do what no penguin has ever done before!
He didn't care what the other penguins said.
Flipper was ready to rewrite history!

As Flipper embarked on his voyage to the mountain,
a friendly face emerged from the sea.
"Hi Flipper." said Flora the orca, "Where are you off to?"

"I am on a mission to achieve my dream!" replied Flipper,
"I'm going to climb the tallest mountain in all the land!"

Flora looked at the mountain and then back at Flipper. "How can someone so small climb a mountain so big? You can't do it.

You are just a penguin."

"Surely you know,

penguins don't climb mountains!"

Before Flipper could reply, Flora swam away.
Flipper was left to contemplate if he had made
the right decision.

All of a sudden, floating in the middle of nowhere, Flipper felt lonely.
The little penguin had never been away from his penguin pals or felt so alone before.

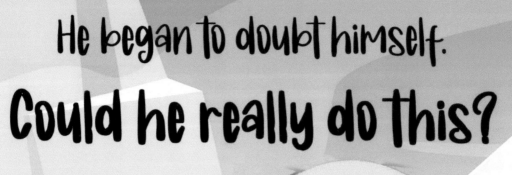

He began to doubt himself.
Could he really do this?

He was going to prove that he could do this, and he would!
He was going to make his dreams come true!

Flipper was strong!

Just as he could see the mountain, the weather took a turn for the worse.

The whirling winds and icy breeze surrounded him. At this point, Flipper considered turning around.

"I could be at home with a warm blanket"
he thought to himself. He couldn't let the weather defeat him!
With the rain dripping off his yellow raincoat, he held onto
his slippery hat and carried on. He was determined to
continue his journey.

As the mountain drew closer, Flipper's heart began to race.
He had never been so excited!

He took an enormous jump and reached the rocky base of the gigantic mountain.

With a deep breath he began his climb.
One flipper after the other.
Up and up he went.
One step closer to the top each time.

"Squarkkkkk!"

Yelled Mr. Beaks the bird, "What is a small penguin doing all the way up here?"

"I am going to the top of this mountain" responded Flipper, knowing that Mr. Beaks was going to try to send him home.

Mr. Beaks went on to tell Flipper:
"Look how high up we are, I have wings,
I won't fall. You might. surely you know...
Penguins don't climb mountains!"

"But I am not an ordinary penguin,
I am Flipper!
I can do this! I don't care what everyone else thinks"
Flipper wasn't going to let anyone stop him again, he was
going to push himself in order to complete this climb. He
was so close. He couldn't give up now!

Flipper was almost there!

He could see the top of this mammoth mountain and he ran to the top...

FLIPPER DID IT!

He jumped with joy!

Flipper saw that he just had to believe in himself.
As long as he listened to his heart,
he could be unstoppable!

Flipper raced back down the mountain.
He was ready to tell the world of his amazing adventure.
He was so excited to tell his family and penguin pals about his climb.

Finally, he fulfilled his dreams and he didn't let anyone stand in his way.

Flipper told his penguin pals and they were so proud! They celebrated for a whole week after his return!

He told Flora the orca and Mr Beaks the bird too! They both had underestimated Flipper and were thrilled for him.

THE END

After completing the amazing climb, Flipper is super hungry! Let's make his favourite snack!

FLIPPER'S FISHY SANDWICHES

Here's what you'll need:
- 1 slice of your favorite bread
- Soft butter
- Cucumbers
- Tomatoes
- Carrots

METHOD

1. Take your bread and butter your slices
2. Cut out the fish shape out of this page and use it as a template to cut the shape of your bread
3. Slice up the cucumbers, tomatoes and carrots in half to resemble the fish scales
4. Places the sliced vegetables on top of the bread to make your fish!
5. Enjoy your tasty treat!

Thank you for helping me make my favourite snack! Remember it's important to have your vegetables to be big and strong!

Cut me out to use as a template for your sandwitch!

What's your dream? You can achieve anything if you put your mind to it. The sky is the limit!

Write your dream here:

....

....

....

....

....

....

....

Special thanks to Dawn Dobney.